CYNTHIA RYLANT

POPPLETON
in Spring

BOOK FIVE

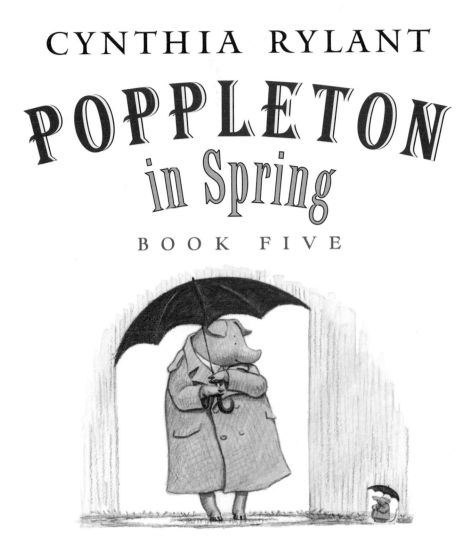

Illustrated by
MARK TEAGUE

SCHOLASTIC INC.

New York Toronto London Auckland Sydney
Mexico City New Delhi Hong Kong

For Donna and Mike Griffith
C. R.

For Zoey
M. T.

This book is being published simultaneously in hardcover by The Blue Sky Press.

ISBN 0-590-84822-4

12 11 10 9 8 7 6 5 4 3 2   9 0/0 1 2 3 4/0

Printed in the United States of America   23

Design by Kathleen Westray

First Scholastic paperback printing, March 1999

CONTENTS

SPRING CLEANING

"It's time for spring cleaning,"
said Poppleton one morning.
He looked around his house.

He had so many things.
Things and things.

There was a box of unmatched socks.

There were jars of old buttons.

One whole shelf was full of rocks.

Poppleton liked his things so much.

But he knew he had to clean.

"I will take some things
to Cherry Sue," he said.
"Then I'll have more room."

8

Poppleton went over to Cherry Sue's
with an armload of things.
"Goodness!" said Cherry Sue at the door.
"Would you like some things?"
asked Poppleton.

Cherry Sue really did not want
some things.
She was trying to spring clean.
But she couldn't hurt Poppleton's feelings.

"Of course," said Cherry Sue.

"We'll put them in my attic."

Poppleton followed Cherry Sue

into her attic.

He dumped all of his things

into a corner.

"I'll sure miss those things,"
said Poppleton.
"I'll take good care of them,"
promised Cherry Sue.

"Wow!" said Poppleton. "Look at
all of that yarn!"

"Yes," said Cherry Sue. "I don't knit
so it just sits there."

"May I have it?" asked Poppleton.

"Of course," said Cherry Sue.

"And look at those thumbtacks!"
said Poppleton.

"I never use them," said Cherry Sue.

"May I have them?" asked Poppleton.

"Of course," said Cherry Sue.

"Hey, a box of shoelaces!" said Poppleton.

Poppleton saw so many wonderful things
in Cherry Sue's attic.

And she was so nice.

She gave him nearly *everything*!

Soon Poppleton's house was
overflowing with things
and Cherry Sue's was clean as a whistle.
Except for a small pile of things
in a corner of the attic.

Poppleton and Cherry Sue had lemonade
in the sun when they were done.
"Don't you love spring cleaning?"
asked Poppleton.

"I love it!" said Cherry Sue.

THE BICYCLE

Poppleton decided to buy a bicycle.

"It will be good exercise,"

Poppleton said.

"I'll get everywhere faster," he said.

"And I'll get to choose a favorite color!"

That was the best part.

Poppleton went to see his friend Marsha
at the bicycle store.

"I would like to buy a bicycle,"
he told Marsha.

"Sure," said Marsha. "What kind
do you want?"
"Just a bicycle," said Poppleton.
"Something for exercise. Something to
get everywhere faster."
"Yes," said Marsha. "But what *kind*?"

She took Poppleton into a big room.
There must have been a hundred
bicycles in that room.

And they were all different.

Marsha showed Poppleton bicycles until
he thought he would faint.
Finally, he pointed weakly.
"That one," he croaked.
"Great," said Marsha. "What color?"

"Red," croaked Poppleton.

"What kind of red?" asked Marsha.

"Red red," croaked Poppleton.

"We have fifteen different kinds
of red," said Marsha.
"Let me show you."
"NOOOOOOOOOOO!!!!!"
screamed Poppleton.

He ran out of the bicycle store.

He ran all the way home.

He got there very fast.

Poppleton changed his mind
about getting a bicycle.
He decided he would just walk.

And anyway, Poppleton was sure now
that if he ever needed to get
anywhere faster —
he'd just RUN!

THE TENT

In spring Poppleton decided
to sleep outside in a tent.
His friends thought he was silly.

"Why sleep outside
when you've got a house?"
asked Hudson.

"Won't you get chilly?"
asked Cherry Sue.

"You'll catch pneumonia,"
said Gus, the mail carrier.
But Poppleton didn't listen
to any of them.

He carried all of his quilts
out to the tent.
He had a flashlight
and a pillow
and some good books.

And long after
everyone else was asleep,
Poppleton was still up.

Sometimes he was reading.

Sometimes he was thinking.

And sometimes he was just
paying attention.

Poppleton loved spring at night.

In the morning, he went
back into his house.
He had a cup of cocoa and
some buttered toast.
Then he went to find Cherry Sue.

He showed her the new flower
that had opened up
while she was sleeping and while
he was paying attention.

Then Poppleton went back inside,
and closed his blinds,
and slept in his bed all day.

"That silly Poppleton,"
said everyone who passed.

Everyone *except* Cherry Sue.